Brother No More

PRAISE FOR *STORYSHARES*

"One of the brightest innovators and game-changers in the education industry."
– Forbes

"Your success in applying research-validated practices to promote literacy serves as a valuable model for other organizations seeking to create evidence-based literacy programs."
- Library of Congress

"We need powerful social and educational innovation, and Storyshares is breaking new ground. The organization addresses critical problems facing our students and teachers. I am excited about the strategies it brings to the collective work of making sure every student has an equal chance in life."
– Teach For America

"Around the world, this is one of the up-and-coming trailblazers changing the landscape of literacy and education."
- International Literacy Association

"It's the perfect idea. There's really nothing like this. I mean wow, this will be a wonderful experience for young people."   - Andrea Davis Pinkney, Executive Director, Scholastic

"Reading for meaning opens opportunities for a lifetime of learning. Providing emerging readers with engaging texts that are designed to offer both challenges and support for each individual will improve their lives for years to come. Storyshares is a wonderful start."
- David Rose, Co-founder of CAST & UDL

Brother No More

Lori Schafer

STORYSHARES

Story Share, Inc.
New York. Boston. Philadelphia

Storyshares
Story Share, Inc.
24 N. Bryn Mawr Avenue #340
Bryn Mawr, PA 19010-3304
www.storyshares.org

Inspiring reading with a new kind of book.

Interest Level: High School
Grade Level Equivalent: 1.7

9781973471899

Book design by Storyshares

Printed in the United States of America

Storyshares Presents

1

We buried Mary on a Sunday. She looked pretty in her best white dress. Mama tied pink ribbons in her black hair. My sweet sister Mary, all wrapped up in pink and white. Like a gift to the angels.

You couldn't see the hole in the back of her head. But we all knew it was there.

It was a nice service. All of Mama's friends came. All of Mary's friends came, too.

None of my friends came. I knew they wouldn't. I was glad they didn't.

A lot of people sent flowers. The workers at Mama's factory. The teachers at Mary's school. Even the kids in the neighborhood. Big bunches of dandelions. They were all that grew in the heart of the city.

Mama arranged them around Mary's grave. Even the dandelions. Mary would have liked that. She thought they were cheerful. Even if they were only weeds.

Mama didn't buy any flowers for Mary. She spent all of her money on the coffin.

"I want Mary to rest in peace," she'd said. "She needs a nice place to sleep."

It was nice. Soft on the inside, and shiny on the outside. Much prettier than Mary's bed at home. But cold. And lonely. The pastor said a few words. About God, and about death.

Then other people started speaking. I didn't listen to them. I was thinking about Mary. And about Mama.

The day before I had found her sitting in the kitchen. She'd had her head in her hands. A stack of bills had sat at her elbow. Rent, and heat, and insurance. But the biggest one was from the undertaker.

"Don't worry, Mama," I'd told her. "I'll help pay for the funeral."

Mama looked up. She'd pushed her chair away from the table. Then she'd stood. She turned to me. She reached out with one hand. She slapped me hard across the face. I let her.

"I don't want your dirty money," she'd said. "And neither does Mary."

I knew she didn't want it. She had never taken it before.

But I needed to do something. I owed it to Mary. It was my fault she was dead.

2

Mama stayed up all night baking pies for the reception. I heard her rolling dough in the kitchen. Near dawn, it grew quiet. I was still awake. I went into the kitchen.

Mama was standing in front of the sink. It was full of dishes. The counter was covered with flour. There were four pies cooling by the window. But Mama wasn't moving.

"Do you want help with the dishes, Mama?" I asked.

She didn't answer me. She kept staring at the sink.

"Are you all right, Mama?"

"Get out, George," she said. She didn't turn around.

I left the room. She didn't try to stop me.

* * *

After the funeral, people came to the apartment. It was filled with the smell of the pies. They smelled good. I loved Mama's apple pies. But I didn't eat any. I left it for our guests.

They stood in our kitchen. They talked quietly to one another. Many of them had been to funerals like this before. The gangs were strong where we lived. Sometimes people get shot. But most of them were young men like me. Not girls like Mary.

No one talked to me. I was glad. I knew they blamed me for what happened to Mary. Maybe they were right.

"That poor, sweet child!" they said.

"Her poor Mama!" they said.

No one said anything about her big brother.

It was after dark when everyone left. I waited outside while they said goodbye to Mama. No one wanted to say goodbye to me. I acted like I didn't care. But I did.

I stood at the window, looking out. I watched the people walking away down the street. The mothers drying their eyes. The fathers with their heads bowed.

Thinking of their own little boys and girls. How it could have been them instead of Mary.

I helped Mama clean up. This time I didn't ask if I could help. I just did it. She still didn't look at me. I didn't look at her, either.

Finally she went and sat down in the living room. I sat down at the kitchen table. For once I had nowhere else to go.

I could hear Mama blowing her nose. I knew she was crying.

She had been crying ever since it happened. Sometimes I didn't think she would ever stop crying.

Sometimes I didn't think I would, either.

3

Mary had just turned twelve. It was nice having a sister who was twelve. She thought her big brother was the greatest guy in the world.

Mama and I liked to tease her about how pretty she was getting. We asked her if she had a boyfriend yet. She laughed at us. Then she ran outside to play ball with the boys.

Most of them were good boys. They were kind to Mary. They were polite to Mama. They did what their parents said. They went to school. They stayed out of trouble.

It was hard to stay out of trouble around here. I never wanted trouble. But it came after me just the same.

I don't know how much Mary knew about me. About who my friends were. About where I went after school. About why I came home so late. About where I got my money.

Maybe she didn't know. Maybe she wasn't old enough to know.

But Mama knew. She hated me for it. She had told me to quit so many times.

"We'll get by," she said. "The Lord will provide."

I laughed at her. Like it was a joke. It wasn't a joke anymore.

I needed the work. Mama barely made enough to feed us. Her friends gave us hand-me-down clothes. Sometimes they didn't fit right.

I could get by. I wore torn blue jeans and an old Army jacket. No one cared. We older boys all dressed the same.

Mama wore a uniform for work. She wore her one dress to church.

But I wanted us to have better things. I wanted that for Mary.

There was always work with the gang. I never knew what the other fellows did. No one talked about it much. But sometimes I would hear about a gas station robbery or a holdup. I would see a police drawing of the suspects on TV. Faces that I knew. Most of the time no one got hurt. But once in awhile someone did.

I would hear guys talking about it. Some of them even seemed to enjoy it. Scaring people, hurting them.

Mama would read about them in the newspaper. "They're scared," she said. "And they're hurt. They want other people to hurt, too."

I didn't know if she was right or not. I only knew I wasn't like that.

I didn't do robberies or holdups. You had to use a knife or a gun for that. I had a knife and I had a gun. But I never wanted to stab or shoot anyone. Not anyone.

Dealing seemed safe. You sold to the people who wanted it. Who needed it. And not to kids, never to kids. At least, I never did.

I thought it was safe. *Who did it hurt?*

I didn't know it would get out of hand. That there would be other gangs who wanted our turf. That we would end up fighting for our part of the city. That someone would get shot because of it.

That it would be my sister Mary.

Mary was gone. Six feet under the ground. In her best Sunday dress. In her church shoes that were shiny but too small. In the nicest, softest bed she ever had.

She would never look at me with those big brown eyes again. They were like the eyes of a deer. Soft, and a little sad.

I will never forget those eyes. Not as long as I live. Mary's eyes.

I see them when I wake up. I see them when I lie down to sleep. I see them when I look at Mama.

But I'll never see those eyes again.

4

The last time I saw Mary was the day she died. I walked Mary to school every morning. Even when I was out late the night before. I usually was.

Mama went to work early. She couldn't take her.

"I'm sorry, George," she said. She was putting on her jacket. "I have to catch the bus at seven."

"I know, Mama," I said. "It's all right. I like walking with Mary."

"She likes walking with you, too." Mama smiled at me. She didn't smile at me very often anymore. Mary did, though.

"Good morning, George!" she said.

I liked it that she still called me George. My friends had another name for me. It wasn't as pretty or as nice.

Mary wore a purple sweater and black jeans. A necklace I gave her for Christmas. And a big, bright smile. The kind she only gave to me.

"Morning, Mary," I said. I smiled back. "Here's your breakfast."

I gave her a plate. She loved my pancakes. I loved making them for her.

"You make the best pancakes, George," she said. She took a big bite. "Even better than Mama's."

"Hush up," I said. I held my finger to my mouth. "Mama will hear you."

Mary giggled. "Mama's at work, silly."

I shook my head. "She has powers," I said. "She knows when you're talking about her."

"Oh, George." She helped me wash the dishes. She told me about her homework. She liked to talk about school. "I have to give an oral report," she said. She made a face. "I have to stand up in front of the whole class to give it."

"You'll do fine, Mary," I said. "I've had to do that. It's not so bad."

"You're braver than me."

"Nah," I said. "I'm just taller."

She laughed and poked me with her elbow.

Mary was brave, I thought. She never acted like she was scared. But I knew she was.

"Are you ready, Mary?" I asked. "Did you brush your teeth and wash behind your ears?"

"George!" she said. She frowned at me. But I could tell she didn't mean it. "I am twelve years old, George. I'm not a little girl. You don't have to remind me all the time!"

"I know," I said. "But I like to."

No, she wasn't a little girl anymore. But I still treated her like one.

I'm not sorry I did.

We walked down the stairs to the street. I reached for her hand.

"Hold my hand, Mary," I said.

She did. Her hand was so small. It was rough from playing outdoors. And tough from helping Mama in the kitchen.

"Let's look both ways before we cross." I always said that. It was like a joke between us. The kind of thing you would say to a little kid.

But I meant it.

Mary nodded. She stopped on the corner. She watched the traffic light.

I watched the men and the cars going by.

Mary never stopped holding my hand while we were walking. She held it until the day she died.

"You're getting so big, Mary," I said as we walked.

Such a big girl. Still holding her brother's hand.

She smiled. I held her hand tighter.

She felt safe with me. It was nice having a big brother. I wished I had one. Someone to look out for me.

I guess I didn't do a very good job of looking out for Mary.

5

It happened late one afternoon. I was out working. Mary always stayed late at the school. She played basketball with the other kids. Then she met Mama at her bus stop. They walked home together.

Mama didn't like Mary walking alone. Mama said Mary was too young to be walking home by herself. I knew that wasn't the reason.

Mary didn't hold Mama's hand like she held mine. I know because I saw them once when they were walking.

Maybe Mary thought she had gotten too big to hold her mama's hand. It was different, holding her big brother's.

If only she had been holding Mama's hand. If only she had been holding mine. It might never have happened.

It was nearly winter. The tree leaves were all dead and brown. The sky was full of clouds. It looked like it might snow soon. And it was cold.

But Mary didn't mind the cold. She never even zipped up her coat. Mama said it was because she had fire in her belly.

The sun set early. It was nearly dark when Mary met Mama at her bus. The snow-clouds made it darker. Mary didn't mind walking in the dark.

"People can't see you in the dark," she said. "It makes you invisible."

Maybe she thought the darkness would keep her safe.

It wasn't a very long walk. A mile, maybe. They were nearly home when Mama bent down to tie her shoe. Mary skipped a few steps ahead.

"Hold up, Mary," Mama called.

"Okay, Mama," Mary said.

She stopped in front of the next apartment building. There was a light on in the apartment on the ground floor.

A man was sitting in a chair by the window. Mary stepped away from the window. She didn't want the man to think she was nosy.

She waited there in the shadows. Mama could barely see her standing on the sidewalk.

I wonder what Mary was thinking as she stood there. If she was scared when she saw that car driving by. If she ducked when she saw the window roll down.

If she saw the gun coming out. If she knew she was going to die.

What was she thinking? Was she thinking about her friends? Was she thinking about a boy she liked? Was she thinking about Mama?

Maybe she was even thinking about me. I won't ever know what she was thinking. No one will.

It wasn't meant for her. It was meant for the man in the apartment. He was supposed to die. Not her. Not Mary.

They probably didn't see her in the shadows. They weren't looking for a twelve-year-old girl. They were looking for a rival. Another gang member. A man who had done them wrong.

But they got her just the same.

By the time Mama reached her, she was already gone. With a bullet in the back of her brain. With her blood all over the sidewalk.

My sister's blood. Mixed with my Mama's tears.

I wasn't there. But I won't ever forget it. Mary lying dead in Mama's arms. Mama screaming and crying for someone to help her. To help her little girl.

No one could help her. Not even her big brother.

I had a gun. I had never used it. I had never wanted to before.

I would have used it then. If I had been there. I would have shot back at those men who shot my sister.

But it wouldn't have done any good. It wouldn't have saved Mary.

6

It happened late one afternoon. I was out working. Mary always stayed late at the school. She played basketball with the other kids. Then she met Mama at her bus stop. They walked home together.

Mama didn't like Mary walking alone. Mama said Mary was too young to be walking home by herself. I knew that wasn't the reason.

Mary didn't hold Mama's hand like she held mine. I know because I saw them once when they were walking.

Maybe Mary thought she had gotten too big to hold her mama's hand. It was different, holding her big brother's.

If only she had been holding Mama's hand. If only she had been holding mine. It might never have happened.

It was nearly winter. The tree leaves were all dead and brown. The sky was full of clouds. It looked like it might snow soon. And it was cold.

But Mary didn't mind the cold. She never even zipped up her coat. Mama said it was because she had fire in her belly.

The sun set early. It was nearly dark when Mary met Mama at her bus. The snow-clouds made it darker. Mary didn't mind walking in the dark.

"People can't see you in the dark," she said. "It makes you invisible."

Maybe she thought the darkness would keep her safe.

It wasn't a very long walk. A mile, maybe. They were nearly home when Mama bent down to tie her shoe. Mary skipped a few steps ahead.

"Hold up, Mary," Mama called.

"Okay, Mama," Mary said.

She stopped in front of the next apartment building. There was a light on in the apartment on the ground floor.

A man was sitting in a chair by the window. Mary stepped away from the window. She didn't want the man to think she was nosy.

She waited there in the shadows. Mama could barely see her standing on the sidewalk.

I wonder what Mary was thinking as she stood there. If she was scared when she saw that car driving by. If she ducked when she saw the window roll down.

If she saw the gun coming out. If she knew she was going to die.

What was she thinking? Was she thinking about her friends? Was she thinking about a boy she liked? Was she thinking about Mama?

Maybe she was even thinking about me. I won't ever know what she was thinking. No one will.

It wasn't meant for her. It was meant for the man in the apartment. He was supposed to die. Not her. Not Mary.

They probably didn't see her in the shadows. They weren't looking for a twelve-year-old girl. They were looking for a rival. Another gang member. A man who had done them wrong.

But they got her just the same.

By the time Mama reached her, she was already gone. With a bullet in the back of her brain. With her blood all over the sidewalk.

My sister's blood. Mixed with my Mama's tears.

I wasn't there. But I won't ever forget it. Mary lying dead in Mama's arms. Mama screaming and crying for someone to help her. To help her little girl.

No one could help her. Not even her big brother.

I had a gun. I had never used it. I had never wanted to before.

I would have used it then. If I had been there. I would have shot back at those men who shot my sister.

But it wouldn't have done any good. It wouldn't have saved Mary.

7

I had to act fast. Everyone knew about my sister. They would leave me alone for a while. But not forever. Soon they would want me back at work.

I wasn't going back to work. Not for them, anyway. Not if I could help it.

I wondered if I could help it.

But at least I had a plan.

My first stop was the barber shop. I sat down in the big chair. I took one last look at myself in the mirror on the wall. The old George. Brother to Mary. Brother no more.

"Cut it all off," I said.

The barber was surprised. "Are you sure, young man?"

"Yes. I want a crew cut." I didn't want a crew cut. I loved my hair. But I needed to look different. A lot different. This was the easiest way.

"All right," the barber said. He still seemed unsure.

He pulled out his scissors. One long heavy dreadlock fell. You could hear it hitting the floor.

"Are you sure?" he said again.

The haircut took half an hour. When it was done, I looked in the mirror again. I was a changed man. I looked like one, anyway.

"My, don't you look different!" the barber said.

"That's the idea," I answered.

I went into an eyeglass store down the street. "Excuse me," I said to the woman behind the counter. "Do you have any plain glasses?"

"Plain glasses?"

"The kind you don't need a doctor's note for?"

"Oh," she said, smiling. "You mean simple lenses. Not prescription."

"Yes."

"We can put them in any frames you like," she said.

"Great, I'll look around." I picked out a large, round pair and put them on. I looked in the mirror. I looked like an owl. "What do you think?" I asked the woman.

"Hmm," she said. "They make you look very smart."

"Perfect," I said. I wasn't sure if my plan was smart. It would be nice if I looked smart.

I stopped at the thrift store next. I needed some new clothes. Button-up shirts and slacks. The kind of clothes you might wear to work. If you had a regular job.

I bought a new jacket, too. A thick, denim one.

Like the kind Mary used to wear. I tried it on in front of a mirror. It made me look younger. But I still felt older.

It was late afternoon when I returned home. I quietly opened the door.

"I'm home, Mama," I called softly.

She might be sleeping. I didn't want to wake her.

She wasn't sleeping. She came into the kitchen slowly. But she jumped when she saw me.

"George?" she said. She couldn't believe her eyes.

"It's me, Mama."

"What have you done, George?" she asked.

I put my bags down on the table. I showed her the clothes I had bought.

"Tomorrow I am going to go out and get a job, Mama," I said.

"Oh, George." Tears came into her eyes.

"I'm going to make you proud, Mama. I'm going to make Mary proud, too."

"Oh, George," she said again.

She put her arms around me. She hugged me and hugged me. It felt good, having Mama hug me again.

She cried. I cried, too. For once we cried together.

I couldn't tell her the whole story. Getting a job was only the first part of my plan. She would have been scared to death if she knew the rest of it.

8

My new job was on the other side of town. In another bad neighborhood. I wanted a job that was far away from my home. I wanted to be where no one knew me.

The job was at a fast food place. The local gangs hung out there. Dealers often met in its parking lot. It was perfect.

Mostly I worked the counter. But I always offered to clear the tables. That was the best way to get information. It took time, a lot of time.

There were a lot of new faces to learn. A lot of new voices and names. But after a while I got to know them. They never paid any attention to me. I did my work and left them alone.

But I listened. Day after day I listened. And I learned a lot about them. Like where they lived. What kind of cars they drove. Who their friends were. And who their enemies were.

Every night I came home late. Mama waited up for me. She would hug me when I walked in. I could hear her sniffing me. She wanted to see if I smelled like fast food. It made her feel better. She was always scared that I might go back to working the streets.

I didn't. And I wouldn't. But sometimes I wished I could.

The job was okay. The people were friendly. My boss was nice to me. But it didn't pay very much. That made it tough for Mama and me. We were barely scraping by. Even without Mary.

I wasn't in it for the money, I told myself. I knew that. But money keeps a roof over your head. Clothes on your back. And food on your table.

I had spent all of my money on a car. I needed one now, to get back and forth to work. I had nothing left for an emergency. What if Mama got hurt and had to go to the hospital?

I tried not to think about that. I had to keep my mind on my plan.

"What's with you tonight, George?" Marissa asked.

She was one of my coworkers. I worked twice as hard when she was on my shift.

I had to. I was always spilling and dropping things when she was around.

"Nothing, Marissa," I said. I smiled at her.

She smiled back. Her smile was like sunshine. It made you feel warm all over.

"You seem distracted," she said.

I shrugged. "Just thinking," I said.

"Well, maybe you should try thinking about the ketchup," she said. She was laughing.

I looked down. I had been filling the ketchup bin. It was so full the packets were falling onto the floor.

I blushed. "Whoops," I said.

My glasses were getting foggy. I pushed them up higher onto my nose.

"Just thinking, eh?" She winked at me. It made her smile look even brighter.

"Say, Marissa," I began. I didn't know what to say. "Um, that's a very nice bracelet you're wearing."

"Oh!" she said. She looked surprised. "Thank you, George. My sister gave it to me for my birthday."

I stopped smiling.

"Do you have any brothers or sisters, George?" she asked.

"Excuse me, please," I said.

I grabbed the box of ketchup packets and walked away. I knew it was rude, but I couldn't help it. Why did she have to ask about Mary?

Mary was the reason I was in this. I couldn't forget that.

I had a job to do here. One that was more important than taking orders and clearing tables. Much more important than talking to girls.

* * *

It was nearly closing time. The place was empty. I went into the bathroom. I cried. I cried for a long time. But I didn't feel any better when I was done.

When I came out of the bathroom, Marissa had gone home. It was just me and Mr. Tanner left. He was the night manager of the restaurant. I could see his gray hair over by the safe. It was his job to count the money before closing.

I helped Mr. Tanner clean up. Then we walked out together.

"You feeling all right, George?" he asked. He stared at me with his deep brown eyes.

"Okay, I guess," I said.

"Nothing you ate here, I hope?"

I guess he noticed how long I was in the bathroom.

"I'm fine, sir."

"Good. You know, I'm very pleased with you, George. You work hard and everyone likes you. I hope you'll stay with us a while."

I dug into my pocket for my keys. I felt funny. No one had ever told me I was a good worker before. It was nice to hear.

"Thank you, sir."

I felt like I should shake his hand or something. But I didn't.

"Well, see you tomorrow." He opened his car door. I opened mine.

"Yes," I said. "See you tomorrow."

That was one other good thing about the job. Having people who looked forward to seeing you again. And not just because of your product.

9

One night, one of the cooks called in sick. When I got to work, Mr. Tanner was frantic.

"George!" he said. "I'm glad you're here."

"Thank you, sir."

"No, George, I need you to work in the kitchen tonight. Think you can handle that?"

"I guess so," I said. "But I've never cooked before."

"That's okay, I'm going to put you on the fryer. It's very simple." He handed me an apron. "You just have to be careful not to get burned."

It *was* simple. The foods were in the freezer. There was a chart on the wall. It showed how much of each food to put in the basket. Three chicken strips. Six fried cheese sticks. A scoop of French fries.

The chart also had times on it. It told you how long to cook each item. All you had to do was set the timer and drop the basket in the oil. You pulled it out when it was done.

Mr. Tanner was right about being careful. I burned my fingers on the basket. The oil splashed a little on my hands. That burned, too.

And it was very hot by the fryer. I spent the whole night sweating. I was glad that Marissa wasn't working.

Around eleven o'clock, business got slow. Mr. Tanner came back to the kitchen to get me.

"Robert can handle it from here, George," he said.

Robert nodded at me. He was the other cook. Very serious, and very quiet. He hadn't spoken to me all night. Except to tell me what to put in the fryer.

"Would you mind cleaning the tables? I'm afraid it's a mess out there."

He was right. The dining room was full of plastic trays and empty drink cups. There was only one table left clean. And sitting around it were the last guys I wanted to see.

It was Snake and his bunch. I had gotten to know them pretty well by now. They were a funny group. They all had animal nicknames. Not all of them were tough, either. One was even called Mouse. He had a high, squeaky voice. But his arms were as big as my thighs!

Snake was their leader. I was pretty sure he had a boss, too. But I had never seen him. Snake usually seemed to be in charge. He wasn't mean, exactly. Just hard.

The other guys were a little afraid of him. It was easy to see why. He was tall in his black boots. He never took off his leather jacket. But you could tell there was no fat on him, only muscle.

He had dark skin and a short thick beard all around his chin. He had a deep voice you could hear from far away. Sometimes I could hear him talking from across the room.

Like tonight.

"He's had it," Snake said. He banged his fist down on the table. It made Rhino jump. "This is the last time. We're taking care of Tiger tonight."

I peeked out from under my glasses. I saw Snake put his hand on a bulge in his coat pocket. His friends did the same.

I felt my heart pounding. I knew Tiger. He stopped in sometimes.

He didn't seem like a bad guy. Not much different from me. A little older. Still a dealer.

And he didn't have a little sister. He did have a daughter. I had heard him talking about her.

"Do you want to go now?" a man known as Goose asked.

"Let's wait a while," Snake said. "He gets in late."   My heart beat faster. Here it was. My big chance. I didn't want to blow it.

"I'm going to take out the garbage, Mr. Tanner," I said. He smiled and nodded at me.

I always offered to take out the garbage. No one else ever wanted to do it. But I wanted to. It gave me a chance to sneak outside for a while. There was a lot to learn outside the restaurant, too.

"Good night, George!" I turned my head. Robin was putting on her jacket. Her boyfriend was standing in the doorway. He always came to pick her up. But I didn't know his name.

"Good night, Robin!" I said.

Her boyfriend nodded to me. I nodded back.

I felt in my apron pocket for my screwdriver. It was there.

I emptied the first trash can. I went to the back door. I walked outside.

I dropped the bag in the dumpster. I began walking slowly back. Snake's car was in its usual spot. My hands were shaking. What if I got caught?

I ducked down and walked up to the car. I bent down to the rear tire. I pulled out my key-chain. It had a tiny flashlight on it. I turned it on. I found the valve where you put the air in. Then I pulled out my screwdriver. I pressed it against the valve until the tire went flat.

"That one's for you, Mary," I said.

Then I hurried back inside.

I had two more loads of garbage to bring out. And two more tires to flatten. I wasn't taking any chances.

I worked more quickly this time. My hands were shaking less. Now it was my knees that were shaking. Squatting on the asphalt was hard.

At last the second tire went soft.

"That one's for you, Mama," I said.

The last one was the hardest. I could see Mr. Tanner turning the lights off in the kitchen. I was worried he would tell the guys to leave before I was ready. He wasn't afraid of them. He was used to them being in the store. They never bothered any of us.

But they didn't know what I was doing yet.

I tried to hurry. It seemed to take forever. The screwdriver slipped in my hand.

Then I dropped the cap. I had to feel around for it in the dark. But I finally found it. I put it back on the last tire. I didnt know who that one was for.

But I smiled as I did it.

I went back inside and washed my hands. Then I started wiping off the counter.

Snake and his gang were getting up to leave.They ignored me, as always. I ignored them, too.

I heard them yelling once they got outside.

"What happened to my tires?" Snake shouted.

"They aren't slashed," Goose said. Just flat.

"Call Leopard," Snake said. He sounded very angry. "Tell him to come pick us up."

"Don't you remember? He went up to visit his aunt and uncle. It will take him hours to get here," Goose said.

"Do you have a better idea?"

I stepped into the break room. There was a telephone in there. It had a private number. There was no way to trace calls from it back to the store.

I pulled out my notebook. It had a lot of names and addresses written in it. They had taken me weeks to get.

I didn't know Tiger's number, of course. That would have been too easy.

But I knew something better. How to reach his landlady. I had looked up the listing for his building a long time before.

"Terrace Apartments," she said when she picked up. She seemed awake. But she sounded mad over being called so late.

I made my voice high, like a girls. "Tiger's in trouble," I said.

"What?" she answered.

"Tiger's in trouble," I said again. "Tell him to take his family and leave town. Tonight."

"Who is this?"

"There's going to be trouble at the apartment," I said in my high voice. "Get him out now."

I heard her drop the phone. I heard a sound like footsteps running away.

And then I hung up the phone.

10

We closed up the store. The manager walked me to my car. He looked a little nervous. Like he wasn't sure if he should leave. Snake and his buddies were still in the parking lot. They still looked mad.

Mr. Tanner sighed. He opened his car door. "Good night, George," he said.

"Good night, Mr. Tanner," I said. "See you tomorrow."

He nodded. I got into my car. I watched him drive away.

Then I cleaned my glasses. I was sweating, and they were foggy.

I pulled out of my parking space. I held tight to the steering wheel. It kept my hands from shaking. When I got to Snake's car, I stopped. My heart was still pounding. But I knew I needed to do this. "Hey, do you guys need a ride or something?" I asked. My voice squeaked. I sounded like a mouse. But I felt like a lion.

Snake looked at me. That was the first time I ever saw his eyes. They were plain and brown. They didn't look like the eyes of a killer. They looked like the eyes of any other man.

He didn't smile. But for a minute he stopped frowning. I guess even the hardest criminals have feelings sometimes. "Nah, we got one coming," he said. "Thanks anyway, kid."

"Okay," I said. "Good night." I rolled up my window. I pulled out of the parking lot. I drove down the street. I thought of them standing there. With their useless car and flat tires.

And Tiger, making his escape. With his wife and little girl. Maybe on their way to a better life. Maybe I was, too. And suddenly I knew who that last tire was for. It was for me.

11

Several days later, Snake and his gang were back at their usual tables. I was listening to them again.

"So, you still trying to get Tiger?" a man asked. I didn't know his name. He had a silver nose ring.

"Nope," Snake said.

My heart dropped. Did that mean they had already gotten him? Maybe my plan had failed after all.

"Nope," Snake said again. "We don't know where he is."

"Did you go to his apartment?"

"His landlady threw him out."

"What?"

"Said he owed three months back rent. She told him to pay up or get out. Now she doesn't know where he is."

I almost laughed. The landlady had thought up a good story for Tiger.

"I guess he owed money to a lot of people," the man with the nose ring said.

"Yeah. She said his mother was sick. Real sick. Big doctor bills." He shrugged. He tapped his finger on the table. "That's what he told me, too. I thought it was a line. Maybe it was true, after all."

I thought I got it then. Snake was Tiger's boss. Tiger hadn't given Snake his cut. That's why Snake was out to get him.

"Well, you're not going to let him slide, are you?" the man with the nose ring said.

Snake shot him a look. "Of course not! He'll turn up sooner or later. And business is business." He tapped his finger on the table again. "But I was thinking I might let him work it off. Just this once." He paused. "Heck, I know how it is. I've got a mother, too."

"What are you thinking about now, George?" said a voice at my elbow.

"Oh, hi, Marissa!" I said. I dropped my cleaning towel. "Nothing, nothing... Just washing the counter."

She flashed that sunshine smile at me. I could feel my face glowing. "You've been washing that same spot for five minutes now," she said.

"Well, Marissa," I said. "Some things are dirtier than others. But if you scrub hard enough, you just might get them clean."

She shook her head at me. I guess I wasn't as deep as I thought I was. But at least she was still smiling.

"You're a strange man, George. Someday I'm going to find out what's going on in that head of yours. You wait and see!"

She nudged my arm with her elbow. She put her hands in her apron pockets. And then she walked away.

I watched her go. *I hope so, Marissa*, I thought. *I hope so.*

12

I got home late again that night. Mama was still waiting for me in the kitchen. For once she didn't sniff me. But she looked very serious. Very serious and very sad.

"Your friend came by today," she said. "Looking for you." She pointed to a note on the table. "He said you haven't been around much."

"No, Mama," I said. "I haven't."

She sat down heavily. She didn't look at me. She looked at the wall instead.

"Are you going back?" she asked.

"I'm going to try not to," I said.

She kept staring at the wall. I stared at it, too.

"Will they let you?" she asked.

"Maybe," I said. "Maybe, because of Mary."

Her back stiffened. Mama and I never talked about Mary. I still heard her crying late at night. Once I had found her in Mary's tiny bedroom, touching her things. But we never talked about it.

"Mary's tombstone is ready," she said to the wall. "They'll put it up next Sunday."

I nodded. I didn't know what to say.

I wished I hadn't mentioned Mary. I didn't want to remind Mama about Mary. Maybe she wouldn't want me around anymore. Like after the funeral.

"Think you can get the day off work?" she asked.

I looked away from the wall. Mama was looking at me. I looked back at her. There were tears in her eyes. There were tears in mine, too.

"Yes, Mama," I said. "I'll be there."

Mary was gone. Six feet under the ground. All wrapped up in pink and white. Like a gift to the angels. I couldn't bring her back. I couldn't take away Mama's pain. I couldn't change what had happened to Mary. I might never forgive myself for what had happened to her.

I couldn't save Mary. But maybe I could save some other little girl. Someone's little daughter. Or little sister.

One less dead little sister. One less tombstone with a little girl's name on it. It would make a man's whole life worth living.

For Mary. May she rest in peace.

She is lovingly remembered by her Mama

And by her big brother George

Who loved her very much.

Brother No More

About The Author

Lori Schafer is a writer of serious prose, humorous romance, and everything in between. More than thirty of her short stories and essays have appeared in a variety of print and online publications. Her first book, *On Hearing of My Mother's Death Six Years After It Happened: A Daughter's Memoir of Mental Illness*, which commemorates Lori's terrifying adolescent experience of her mother's psychosis, was published in November 2014.

About The Publisher

Story Shares is a nonprofit focused on supporting the millions of teens and adults who struggle with reading by creating a new shelf in the library specifically for them. The ever-growing collection features content that is compelling and culturally relevant for teens and adults, yet still readable at a range of lower reading levels.

Story Shares generates content by engaging deeply with writers, bringing together a community to create this new kind of book. With more intriguing and approachable stories to choose from, the teens and adults who have fallen behind are improving their skills and beginning to discover the joy of reading. For more information, visit storyshares.org.

Easy to Read. Hard to Put Down.

Made in the USA
Middletown, DE
20 January 2023

22705210R00045